SKULLS
WITH EYEBALLS
IN THEM

SKULLS WITH EYEBALLS IN THEM

A Specimen Book

~ Featuring ~
The disestablished and uncorroborated drawings of
Barn Quivver MacAnüs

StarHouseBooks

Skulls With Eyeballs In Them - A Specimen Book,
Featuring the disestablished and uncorroborated
drawings of Barn Quivver MacAnüs
Illustrated by X-W for Star House Books
starhousebooks.com
All illustrations © 2023 X-W. All other art, design,
and text © 2023 Star House Books
ISBN: 9798870248387
Imprint: Independently published
Printed by Kindle Direct Publishing

for Heidi
the only real artist I've ever met
magnet
firestarter
magician
the love of my life

About the Artist

Little is known about these drawings and their purported creator Barn Quivver MacAnüs. The content positioned as the "Foreword" in this edition is the only known documentation to bear his name or signature.[1] Genealogical records for the Northern Scottish Isles before the seventeenth century are either lost or never existed in the first place. The latter is most likely due to the fact that the Islands were isolated, remote, and somewhat famously populated by "the most ill-humored, cantankerous, and frightful peasants one shall ever meet, with no love of outsiders and an uncanny handiness with pitchfork and carving knife."[2] There is no entry in the Big Book of Families for a Clan of MacAnüs. Oral histories from as late as the 1700s say the Nor'easter Isle communities survived by barter, their own network of sea-faring trade, and piracy. It appears they had little use for the Crown's legal tender and therefore were unofficially allowed to remain in effect, self-governing, with nominal if any taxation.

Efforts to prove the existence of the artist/father/husband/brother/alleged eater of human flesh known as Barn Quivver MacAnüs have, for this publishing team, been fruitless. Most academics and genealogists refute the small body of evidence as either:

a) ephemeral detritus that has been mis-attributed and therefore ultimately misleading

b) an outright hoax perpetrated by parties unknown for unknown gain

As well, the numerous references to a heretofore innominate race of ancient ghouls who scoured medieval battlefields consuming the remains of fallen soldiers—defies any rational explanation other than as a fairy tale, a regional colloquialism shared with a wink and a nod, or a ghost story told around an evening's campfire.

• • •

That said, the words "hoaxer", "charlatan", "mountebank", and "bunco artist" have been found in the same sentence when speaking of one Doon Barn Manus (presumably an unintentional or intentional misspelling of the surname). This name does appear in several *gaol* or *jaile* logs in the Aberdeen and Dundee areas per the late 1480s. Accusations ranged from petty theft and *Thompeeping,* to the more curious charge of "defiling and gnawing the beatific remains of a Holyman recently deceased". The District of Bankside Prison's ledger entry for June 9, 1489, states that a 'Doon B. Manus, though young, died whilst incarcerated'.[3]

---

[1] The Moribund, publicly known as a merchant ship but inexplicably armed with 48 cannoned turrets, was rumored to be a private warship for hire. The passenger manifest circa 1480 counts one B.Q. "Seamus" MacAnüs as a "working guest-mate, handy in the galley and the morgue". Adding to the ship's reputation for clandestine voyages, she never carried an official scribe on any campaign, and thus we have no way to assign identity to this "guest-mate". It's quite possible that a completely unrelated party signed the registration with a nickname or pseudonym.

[2] Lloyd & Goeckner, 1669

[3] Notation Line 5; "The lad revealed his own self to be a purveyor of rotted flesh and bore an undowsable anger within his soul. T'was dispatched with oil and flame by the Keep's Undertaker and galley-mates."

Publisher's Note

Most often a book's front matter, and in particular the official note from the publisher, is a celebration of the heart, soul, blood, sweat, and tears—in a word, the *teamwork*—required to create a book. Occasionally though, and fortunately quite seldom, the 'Publisher's Note' is required to act as a disclaimer, a caveat, or an outright denial of the veracity of the publication's contents.

That said dear reader, duly note: The following 'documentation' that has been parlayed into what amounts to the Foreword quite simply, could not be verified by our research and archive staff. Thus, all 'historical data' referenced within these pages is suspect, and per our inability to determine otherwise, lacks any valid evidential proof.

Putting the source material's existential crisis aside, the gist, or *spiritus objecti* of this book, is of course the stylistically wild, varied, and often comical drawings of skulls (and eyeballs).

"There, but for the grace of God, go I." -Proverb

These drawings may, as the artist said, "...exist only as an entertainment". Or should we all accept our individual fates to be unknown, any one of these illustrations could be a portrait of our future selves. A portentous reminder indeed, and as Picard once recommended, "Make now always the most precious time." With that in mind, we present to you this collection of the dreaded *cerebrumus cum oculus*.

From the first known publication, 1482

Translated from the original Manx, date unknown

These Publisher's & Book Maker's Notes:
The following fore-word scriptures, in the form of three hand-crafted parchments and numerous drawings, were duly provided to us by one Dooner Phalli MacAnüs the Younger, of Netherstown, Pindik Farth, Scotland, properly known to be the lone blood son of, and only living known kin to, the artist of this book's pages, one Mr. Barn Quivver MacAnüs, deceased.

The property and rights of said artworks on these pages, and the public notations within this Foreword, are hereby acknowledged to have been paid for and purchased by us, though once formally the property of, as well as a conversation in privy, a-tween members of a family, namely Father and Son. Thus said, all words and works have been properly permissioned to us, the publishers, Twinecock Bros. Ltd., by Young Master Dooner himself, who was under no amoral influence or known to be in an inebriated state upon signing his transfer of permissions to us the publishers. For these papers and drafts he has been duly paid in both coin and privileged passage from our Norther Port, upon the next sailed voyage of his own choosing.

All of this, the above and following partook and witnessed Saturday, 8 November, 1482, before his departure to sea and exodus from the Isle of Scot. So here now this document shall be legally binding in his absence.

On this day with this document we bear permission for the following artistic works to be printed, bound, and distributed for purchase by any commoner, smithy, or Royal, here in the highlands and further out as we are able, to mainland and sea islands, to the goodly peoples of the lowlands, to cottars and crofters alike, weather permitting.
Signed and Noterlain on this day of Diluan-Monday, 10 November, 1482

Clarence Son C. MacGonad

Clarence Son Cannor MacGonad

With Witness on this very day,

Duncan Jörn MacWeeny

Duncan Jörn MacWeeny

Foreword

1916 Translation from the original Norse-Galeic, dates unknown

To me young Boy Dooner,

I find meself upon a ship delayed by turgid seas. I am bound for our home of Scot, but the bloated wash impedes our arrival. And hear me this; I am but ill. The cook-mate, who is also the doctor and amputist, declares me fever and boils to have resulted from "something ye eated". More to the likely, the fester of fleas about me loins and the ticks all about me head will soon bite deep and begin to ravage me from within. I feel this is me demise, and an injustice; for as you know, a lifetime have I spent in the Lord's calling. I labored for the benefit of all man, woman, and child. Dutifully and faithfully have I followed the warring legions across the seven seas and lands, and once the killing was finished, I helped rid the world of dead and their diseased flesh. And yet by God's hand here I am, weakened in me old age, left to die from the sickening bites of ten thousand tiny vermin.

By Captain's order I have been sequestered to the orlop and have naught but old ropes, stewage, and rats for company. So is rightly done for the welfare of this ship's crew. Truly I am a pariah and I have no argument with me confinement. I count me blessings, for a colder-hearted man would have thrown me to the briny deeps.

The slag-boy kindly brings me scrappings from the mess, but lays them on the floor at the foot of the stairs, more than a fall from where I lay. Each bowl has toppled and spilt from the swells, but he brings me new every day just the same. As I have said, no longer handy am I, and truly also, even unable to crawl. As well too, my spirit is so far weakened that I cannot right myself proper for me own evacuation, and thus I lay here in a corner, with naught but a tin lamp and me papers, sodden in me own waters and shite.

Should I not live long enough to see the shores of our beloved Stroma, where I'm a-hoping ye and kin still mind the turret and sailor's light, I have bargained no less than two hale and hearty mates on this vessel, and both have sworn their oath to me: Should me spirit leave to Heaven afore I am home, oneth or t'other will service and journey to ye at the lamptower, to furnish ye this letter along with me trunked and laggard tydings.

· · ·

Day 2, hear me wishes I write to ye, Boy Dooner: Aghast I are, for upon this moment me realizes ye must be more man than boy now. And I know yer mum has raised ye straight and goodly. Me work, me destined duty in service of the Lord and all men, has taken me far from home for many seasons. More than I trusted all those years ago. On this day I regret our lives spent apart.

My wish for ye, me young lad, is that ye'll not follow in me footsteps. I wish for ye a life on land, surrounded by the love of kin and village. For ye I wish all I had not.

Old fool I be, but here me tell ye, a man of yer age would do well to walk out to the knolls, and in a quiet place a-listen to the sky. A-listen to the dirt and sea. For a truth I can tell ye, even a good man's heart grows heavier with age. A man cannot know his own worth, to himself and his kin and love-kind, but familiar hands to hold ye close, and honest work, those be greater than glory or gold.

Now some men, and once a rare whiles a woman too, will be deaf to the song of their own soul. Should ye meet one of such a kind, flee for yer life and all ye hold dear. They will speak sweet and make simple the world for ye, and afore ye know it they'll soon lay shame upon ye for not tiding to the 'proper' work for a man of our kind. For to them, yer life is theirs to squander. To hell and their grandfather's sheep, I say. Should ye take a sit and quite yerself, ye'll know yer life is yer's alone.

Even since the first-borns Cain and Abel rivaled, the world has been a-warring. And ever since the world has warred, our kind have given their service. But I say to ye Dooner, ye are not obliged to answer the song of that siren as yer ancestors and me and our likes have done.

Though God made ye and our kind with such a purpose, ye owe not yer life to the world, aye and not even God would ask ye for it. Heretical that ain't, though it might burn some ears to hear it. But I have seen the world, laddie, and God is love and He will give ye a gift, but never command ye use it, nor to witness as I have the hard and hating works of man. Me travels, by foot and ship and wheel, following country to country, war to war, has brought me to this end here today: Dismayed by man's appetite for destruction, poisoned and filthy, and heartsick for home. Given me druthers I'd give back all the gold and glory for just one day, sunny or dark t'would be no matter, to sit at table with ye and yer marm.

Be not mistaken, there are still those in the world who are grateful for the work that we and the others-kind do. They pay an honest coin, whilst their young would rather chase us off. Any village or kingdom that has known a fight will understand that we and our kind were made by Him The Creator, the Good Lord Himself, to eat the dead after battle.

The olden folk I have met on my trails, whether by hill or cobble street, know of us, and know the work we have done since the beginning, since we lived in The Garden alongside the first-borns.

But here now today is the modern world. Wrought changes in me own lifetime. The young, those yer gauge and younger, they fear and bigot us. There are those of the young who'd rather dig holes in the ground—everywhere—to bury the dead rather than have us eat them clean and neat. Can ye imagine, the beautiful winded lands of home riddled with grave marks and headstones of all the many who perished in battle?

I fear now I have become a relic. Perhaps the youngsters are right and the ceremony of place and remembrance has rightfulness. I cannot separate me own way of thinking, me love for the idylls and clear green hills, from what these so younger may hold for right or wrong. Old I am, I deny it not, yet laugh for I've been put out of my living by a shovel and a strong back! Still, me breast is prideful. For millennia, we the *luchd-ithe bàis*, have kept the world safe of fester, rot, and disease. Always impartial, always without allegiance to skin, creed, or the folly and hubris of one warring faction over another. That is as God gave us the teeth to do. For eons the masters of war have throwed their children upon the Reaper's scyth, and for eons our kind, we ate them all.

• • •

Day 3, in haste: hear me Dooner,
With regard to all ye may find within the trunk and in particular me drawings on paper. I know they are curious and may strike ye a-weird. Know true they exist only as an entertainment and have no arcane purpose beyond a laugh at the devil and to shake a fist at our last breath.

These drawings were born of the fatigue and waiting for a battle to end. The gathering of our kind so follows each battle and we waits some distance apart, camped upon a hill or cluster in a sallow or copse, patient for the last of the vanquished to fall, patient for the weary victors to abandon the field. For us *luchd-ithe*, a gentle occupation to pass the time is required. Not a-one of us could sit about for days and nights as the swords ring and the mothers weep.

Certainly we could not make merry, nor eat or drink before we'd begin the gorging. The wails of crime and cruelty that is warfare, aye, they sickened us all. Each of us in camp partook a way to pass the time. Some tended their garments, some tended their children (yes, even the babes would soon eat heartily) some worked a craft of hand. Me, for reasons unbeknownst to meself, I chose to draft. As a boy, I heard tell of one great-auntie with a knack for putting charcoal to parchment. Perhaps I was born with some of her within me.

Some years ago on a day of sunlit autumn, the oaks were red and the sky black as the bloodied ground. And so I sat a-resting after me day's first meal. With pen and paper in hand, I was noting to me brother, yer uncle Celeg. I was a bit weary in me head and without intent, and so me mind began to wander. Soon me hand and pen followed and I found on me paper that I'd drawn a mockery of a half-dead mucker. I recognized him to be a Boolean Warrior I'd eaten earlier that very morning! He himself was lying atop a plonk of his fellen brothers and him with his flesh all burnt off and him with one eye still perched in its hole like a robin's egg in a nest.

Me bunk-mate sitting a-stride me at the campfire looked upon me draw and laughed the laugh of a goose on Sunday morning. He stripped the page from me hands and strode about the camp, showing it to all. Soon the camp was laughing a howl, and me myself as well. After that day, a tinkering lad or even a mum with babe would come a-calling on me, and ask for a draw, always the likeness of a one-eyed deadman. Each day that I dipped me pen, I still strove to write to you and the homefolk, but instead I'd fall into a trance, making a scribe to fit someone's desire, always in the likeness of a skull & peeper.

To be frank-spoken, I didn't mind the distraction, and as well, I rather enjoyed to see the smiles that me markings borne. These works did keep me from a-writing to ye and our kin, which to be frank again, often put in me a somber, for I hurt with a sickness for home. Me days then were both goodly and badly.

After that and a bit time more, at each new battlefield I was quick to take notice of such apparitions and I found them to be common. Country to country, battlefield to battlefield, any number of one-eyed dragoons could I find. Many I found were crammed deep under cairn-like piles of limbs and battlements. Others lay about and underfoot, torn from their flayed bodies, just a-gazing up at the sky.

Some days I'd not even eat me fill of soldiers for want of wandering the moors with hopes to sight a fleshless dome housing a single orb. Also too, any number of camp-mates would spy an *aon sùil* and bring it to me for reproduction. Through grey winters and muddy rains, a rich parade of decimated craniums kept our spirits high.

For some years now I have made many-a mark and emptied many a quill pot. For each one that I gifted to a grateful friend, I would effort to draw one for meself as well. These ye will find within the trunk, bound with cheesecloth and twine.

So, my dear Dooner, if we are never to embrace arms again, and today I feel it will be so, I pray that me brothers at sea will honor their words, and anon, this letter will find ye.

All me worldly treasures reside within the trunk and as such, I bequeath all to ye and to ye alone. Now is me shame that their worth is naught more than a mouse's arse.

And though me life be founded on noble means and gifts from the Lord on High Himself, alas, I must say to you, I feel the noble duty of me calling was not worth the absence of yer hearts. I pray ye learn from me sorrows and know ye I ask not yer forgiveness, for no, I deserve it not.

Ann an gaol,

Yer Father Barn

p.s.

Within the trunk folds ye will find a clay-sculpted donkey, 'tis from the isles of Vanuatu. Me hopes he may bring a whit of charm and grace to the four-pane window of yer mother's kitchen. From me soul to yer lips, tell her I love her.

"The Reaper's glass be freshly turned,
shined oak and sandy swirls.
Anon for you now little boys,
make haste ye little girls!"

~Traditional sea chanty

FIGURES

fig. 1
Seamus

fig. 2
The Beguiler

fig. 3
The Frenchman

fig. 4

The Gottendamnit

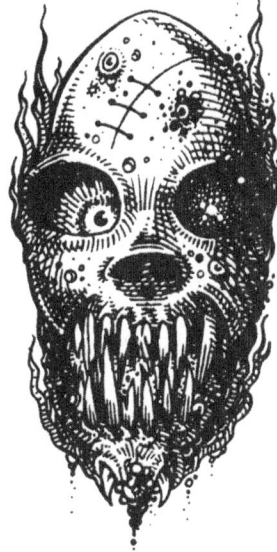

fig. 5

The Scaredycat

fig. 6

The Submissive Tinkler

fig. 7
The Sniffer

fig. 8
The Restless Soul

fig. 9
The Candy Eater

fig. 10

The Welp

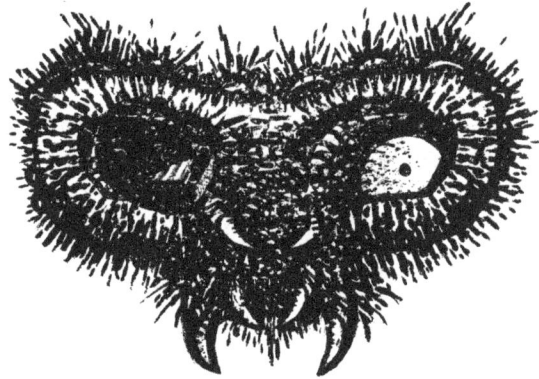

fig. 11

The Poop Head

fig. 12

La Cassarolé

fig. 13
The Polecat

fig. 14
The Crusher

fig. 15
The Bonehead

fig. 16

The Gullible

fig. 17

The Frankinfarter

fig. 18

The Swampy One

fig. 19
The Muckraker

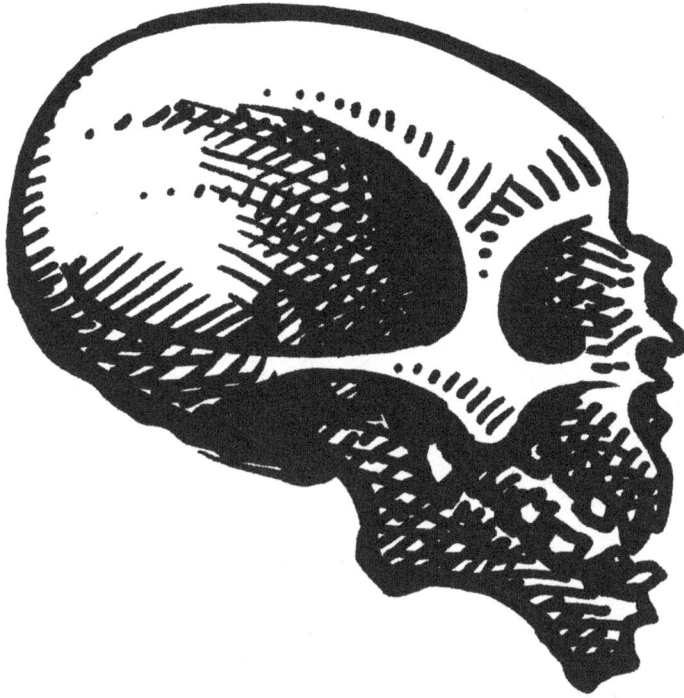

fig. 20
The Grunter

fig. 21
The Yeller

fig. 22

The Klepto

fig. 23

The Bird Brain

fig. 24

The Plugger Upper

fig. 25

The Mollycoddler

fig. 26
The Executioner

fig. 27
The Stinger

fig. 28

The Freakazoid

fig. 29

The Blockhead

fig. 30

The Buddha's Younger Brother

fig. 31
The Snapper

fig. 32
The Boobface

fig. 33
La Cheri Amour

fig. 34

The Stool Pigeon

fig. 35

The Cookie Eater

fig. 36

The Scooter

fig. 37
The Flunky

fig. 38
The Will o' the Wisp

fig. 39
The Hermit

fig. 40

The Looker

fig. 41

The Kiester

fig. 42

The Butt Munch

fig. 43
The Sourpuss

fig. 44
The Ornery

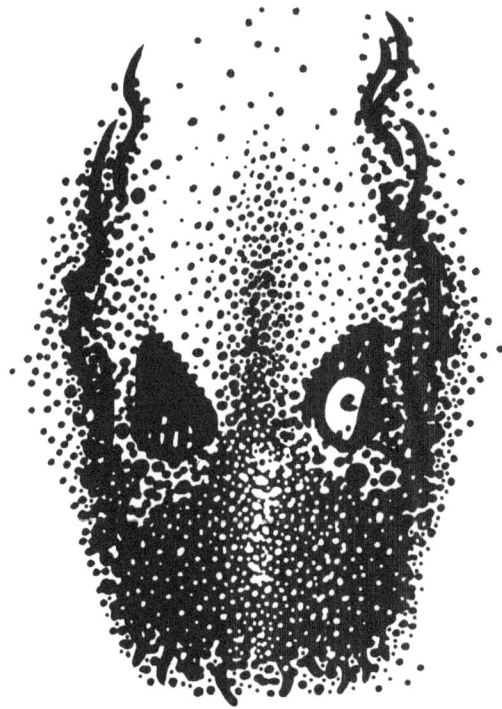

fig. 45
The Flautist

fig. 46

The Nard Kicker

fig. 47

The Grits

fig. 48

The Well-Bathed & Often Charming

fig. 49
The Rooster

fig. 50

The Continental

fig. 51

The True Believer

fig. 52
El Guapo

fig. 53
The Snorker

fig. 54
The Scheister

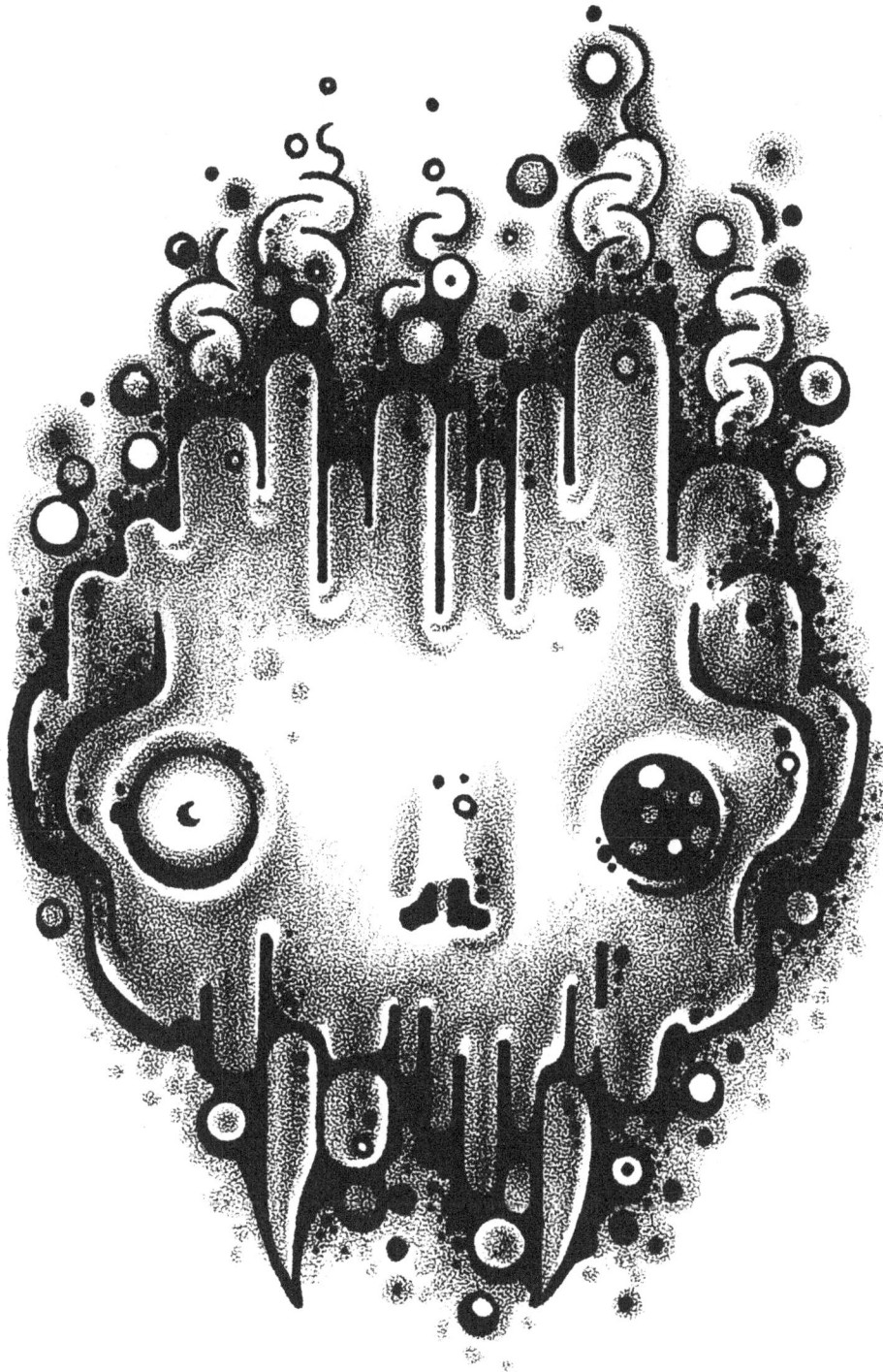

fig. 55
The Balogna Thrower

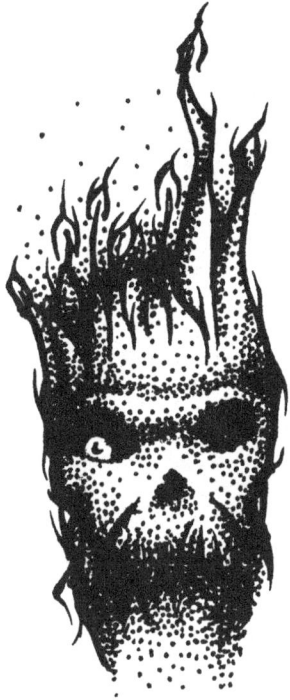

fig. 56
The Tootster

fig. 57
The Loaf Pincher

fig. 58

The Rabbit of Caerbannog

fig. 59

Mr. No Cojonés

fig. 60

The Colon Log Cutter

fig. 61

The Squeaker

fig. 62

The Shorthose

fig. 63

The Sausage Maker

fig. 64

The Wang Dang Doodler

fig. 65

The Hapless Dolt

fig. 66

The Very Disappointed

fig. 67

The Moron

fig. 68
The Haggered

fig. 69
The Kibitzer

fig. 70

The Milquetoast

fig. 71

The Krampus

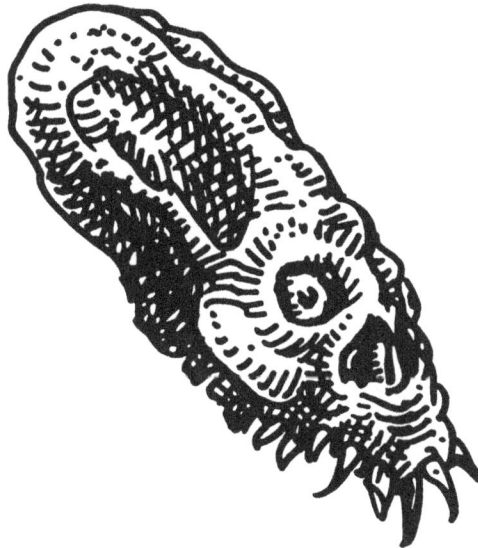

fig. 72

The Stewed In Their Own Juices

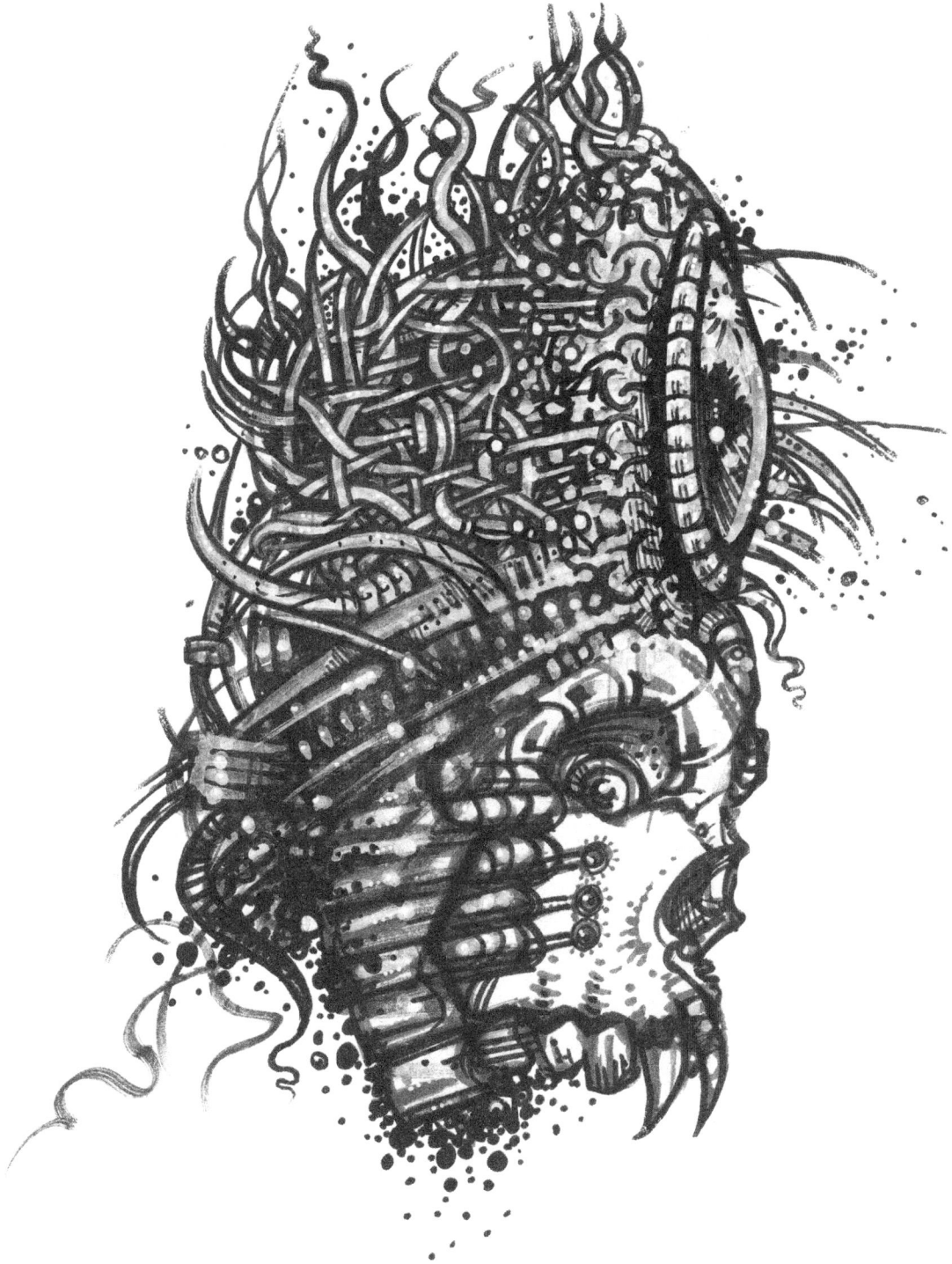

fig. 73
The Schlemiel

fig. 74
The Obliterator

fig. 75
The Mortified

fig. 76

The Spanker

fig. 77

The Just Ducky

fig. 78

The Xenophobe

fig. 79

The Yapper

fig. 80
The Licker

fig. 81
The Biter

fig. 82

The Blubber Butt

fig. 83

The Pee-Wee

fig. 84

The Schlemazel

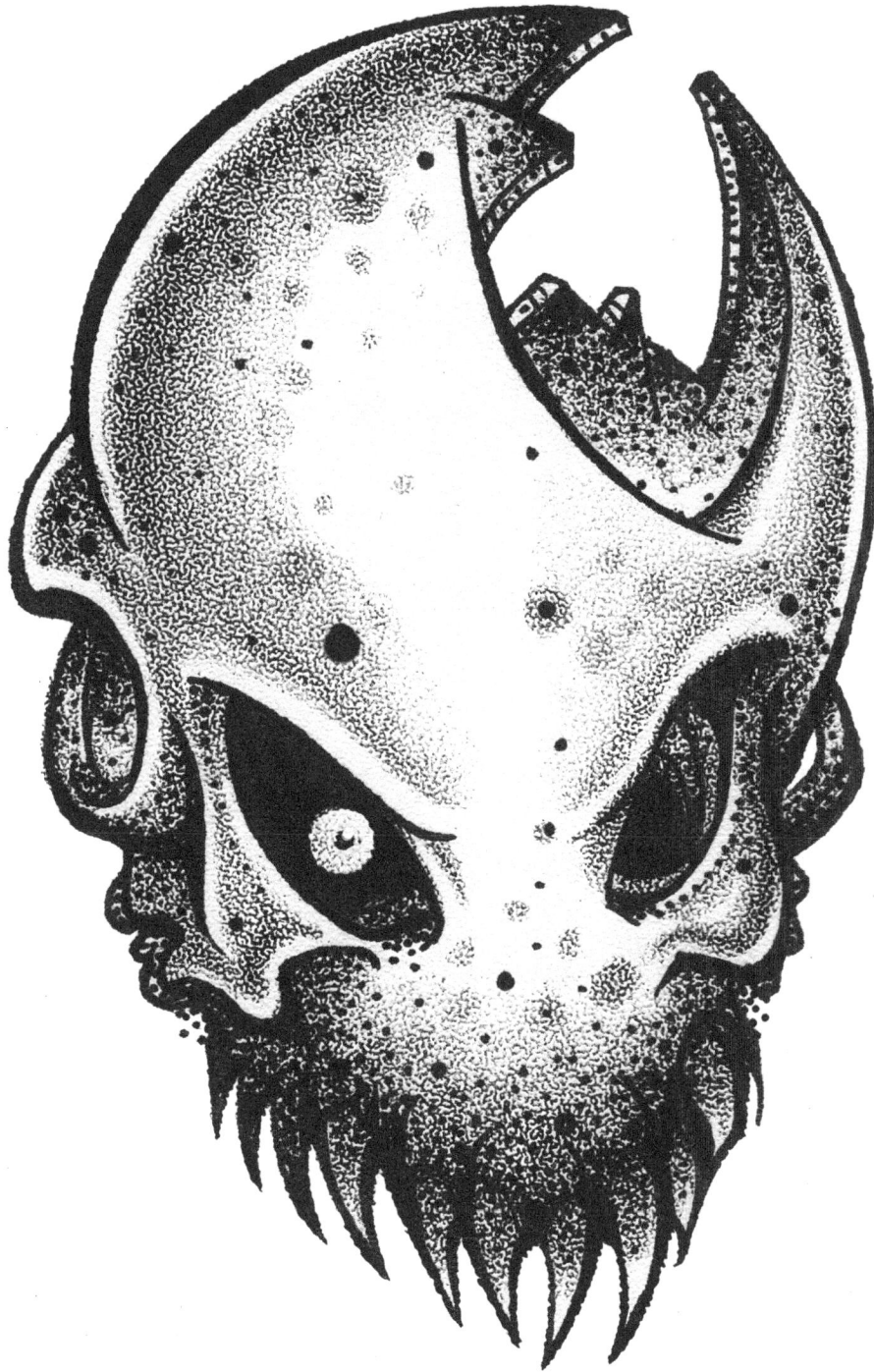

fig. 85
The Lemmy

fig. 86
The Halford

fig. 87
The Ball Breaker

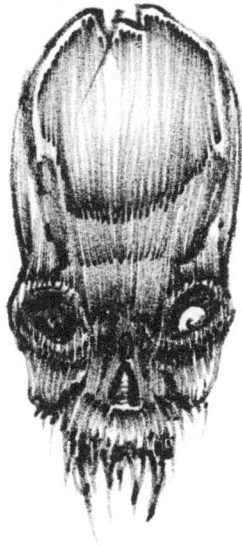

fig. 88

The Pants Pooper

fig. 89

The Ninny

fig. 90

The Knifer

fig. 91

The Nincompoop

fig. 92
The Wolverton

fig. 93
The Axer

fig. 94

The Dingleberry

fig. 95

The Wiener

fig. 96

The Bludgeoner

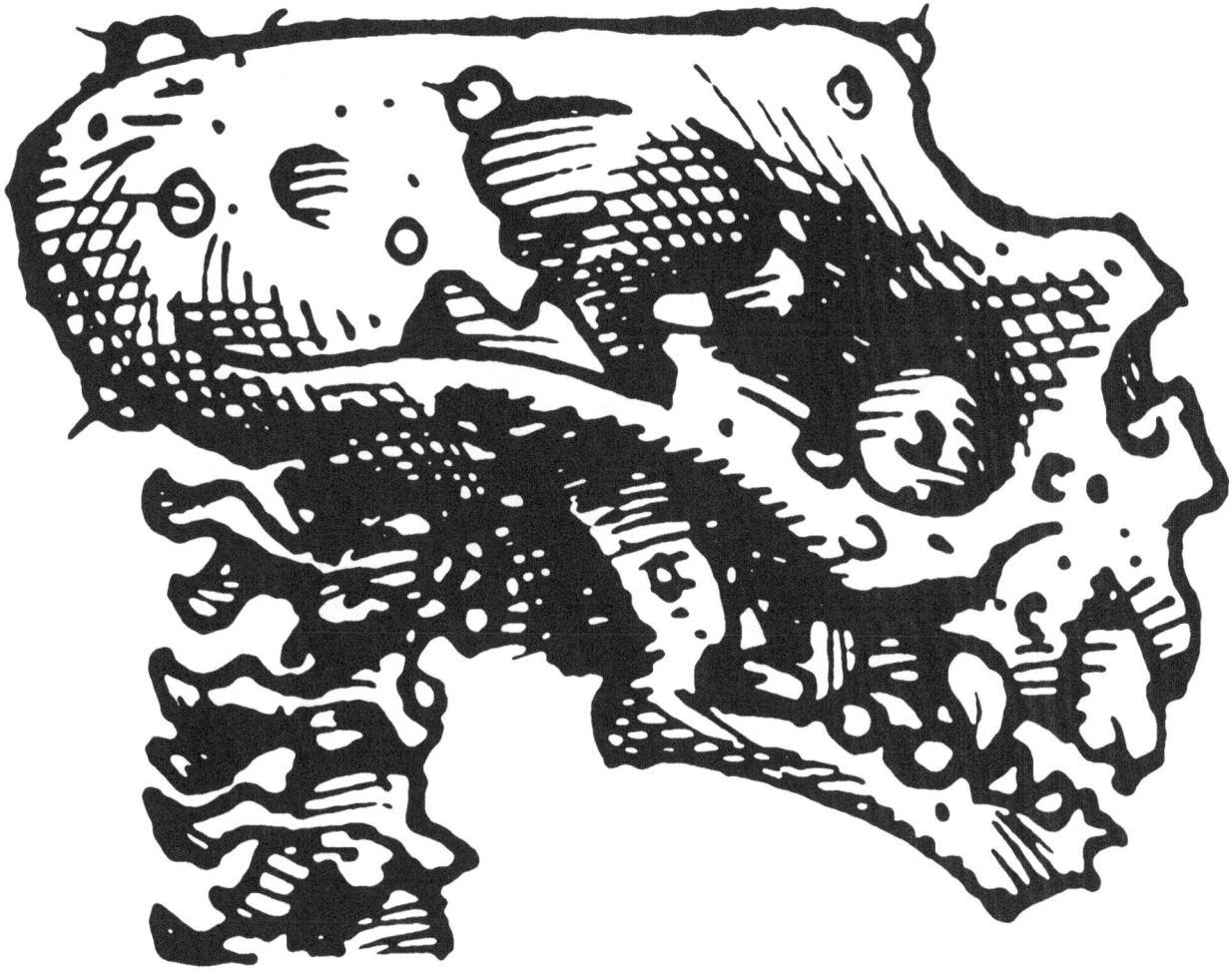

fig. 97
The Harpy

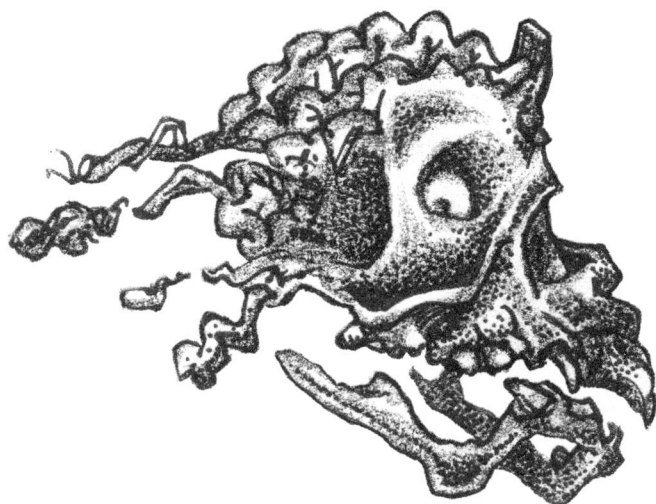

fig. 98
The Jackass

fig. 99
The Philthy

fig. 100

The Ankle Biter

fig. 101

The Doofus

fig. 102

The Mikkey

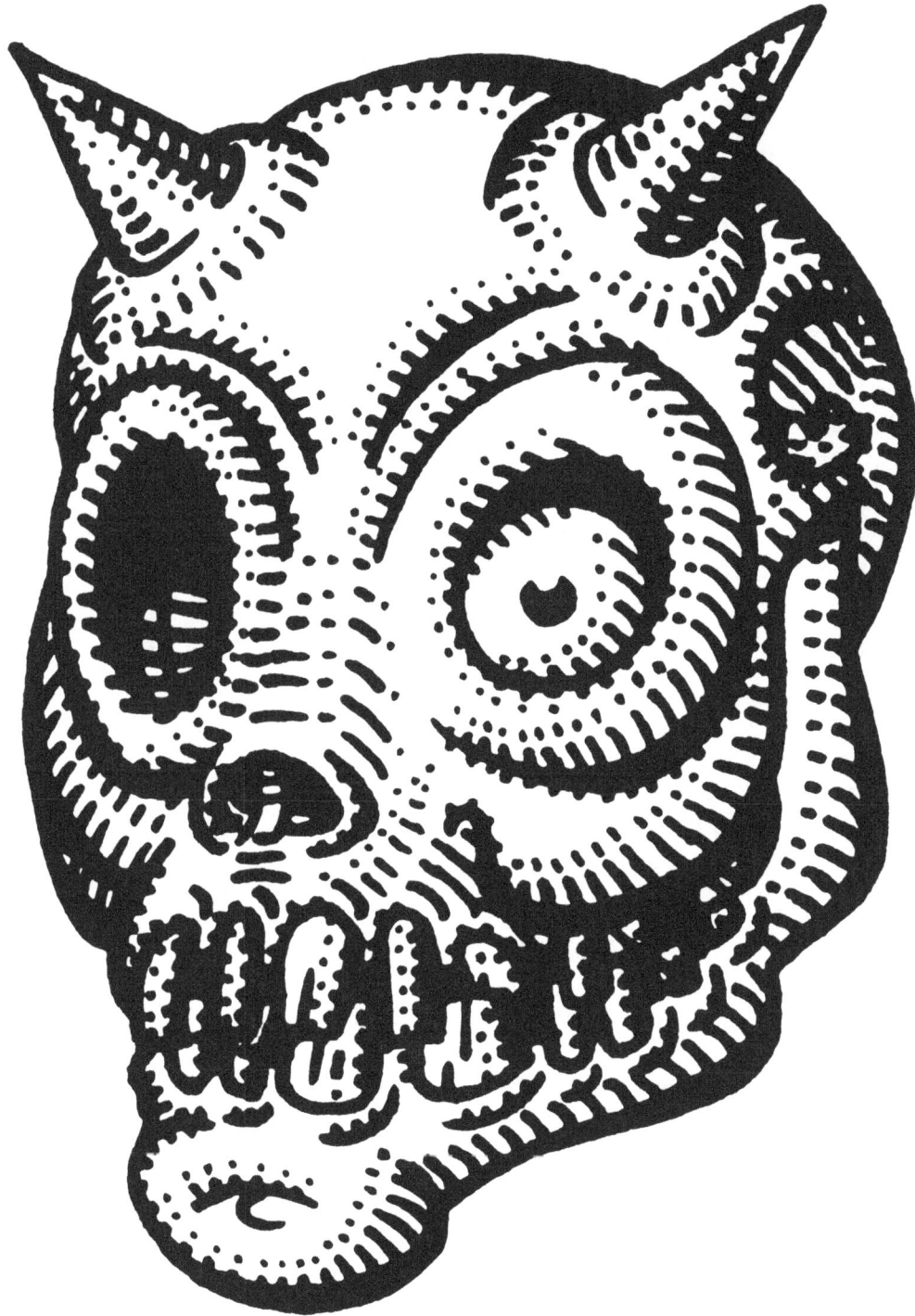

fig. 103
The Wizzö

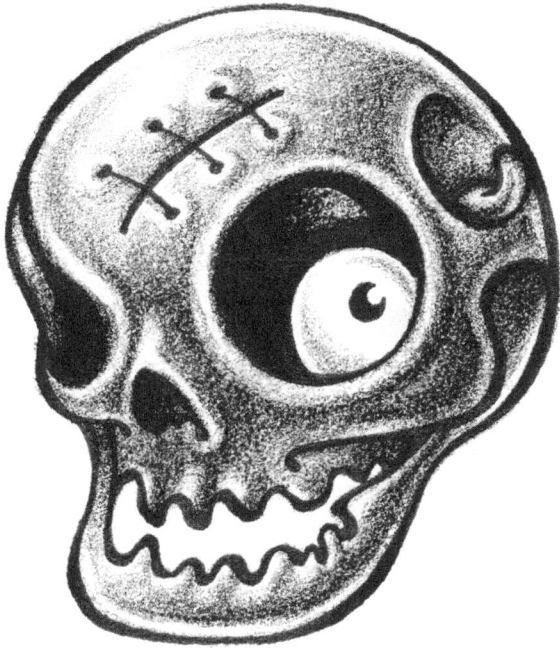

fig. 104

The Scatterbrain

fig. 105

The Fast Eddie

fig. 106

The Burgermeister

fig. 107

The Würzel

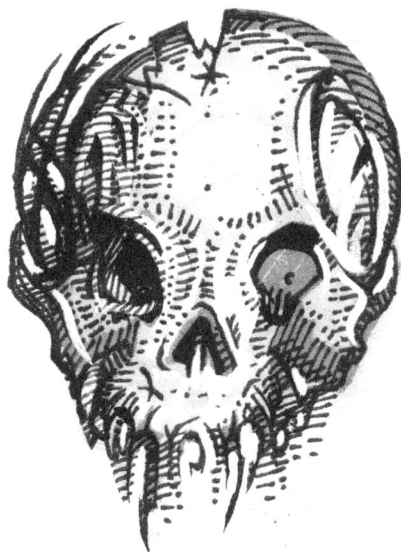

fig. 108

The Bradbury

fig. 109

The Martian

fig. 110

The Dullard

fig. 111

The Rooster

fig. 112

The Chest Thumper

fig. 113

The Masher

fig. 114

C'est la Shite

fig. 1
The Child

About the Typefaces

Cormorant Garamond

Designed by Christian Thalmann
Cormorant is a type family developed by Christian Thalmann, Zurich, Switzerland.
Cormorant was conceived, drawn, spaced, kerned, programmed, interpolated, and produced in its entirety by Christian Thalmann.
Cormorant fonts are available via Google Fonts.

Licensed under the Open Font License.

Lexend

Designed by Bonnie Shaver-Troup, Thomas Jockin, Santiago Orozco, Héctor Gómez, Superunion Design
The Lexend typefaces were designed for optimal readability and to improve reading performance for readers of all ages and ability.
Lexend fonts are available via Google Fonts.
www.lexend.com
Licensed under the Open Font License.

About Kindle Direct Publishing

Kindle Direct Publishing allows authors and artists to self-publish eBooks, paperbacks, and hardcover books for free. The platform provides options to expand availability on a global scale, making independent creatives' work accessible to readers around the world.

About Star House Books

Adelheide S. and William G. are the owners of Star House Books, a small publishing house located in Portales, New Mexico, USA. A life-long love of words and pictures (not necessarily in that order) compelled them to found the company in 2023.

SHB publishes an eclectic variety of books, most recently *The Major Arcana Coloring Book*, and *The Celtic Knots Coloring Book*, both featuring exclusive original drawings and designs by the artist Ashley Fern. For more information visit www.starhousebooks.com

Index

StarHouseBooks

www.starhousebooks.com

Made in the USA
Monee, IL
19 December 2023